The Fox and the Crow

Based on a story by Aesop

Retold by
Mairi Mackinnon

Illustrated by
Rocío Martínez

Reading Consultant: Alison Kelly
Roehampton University

Fox was always hungry.

3

One day, he
saw Crow...

...with some cheese.

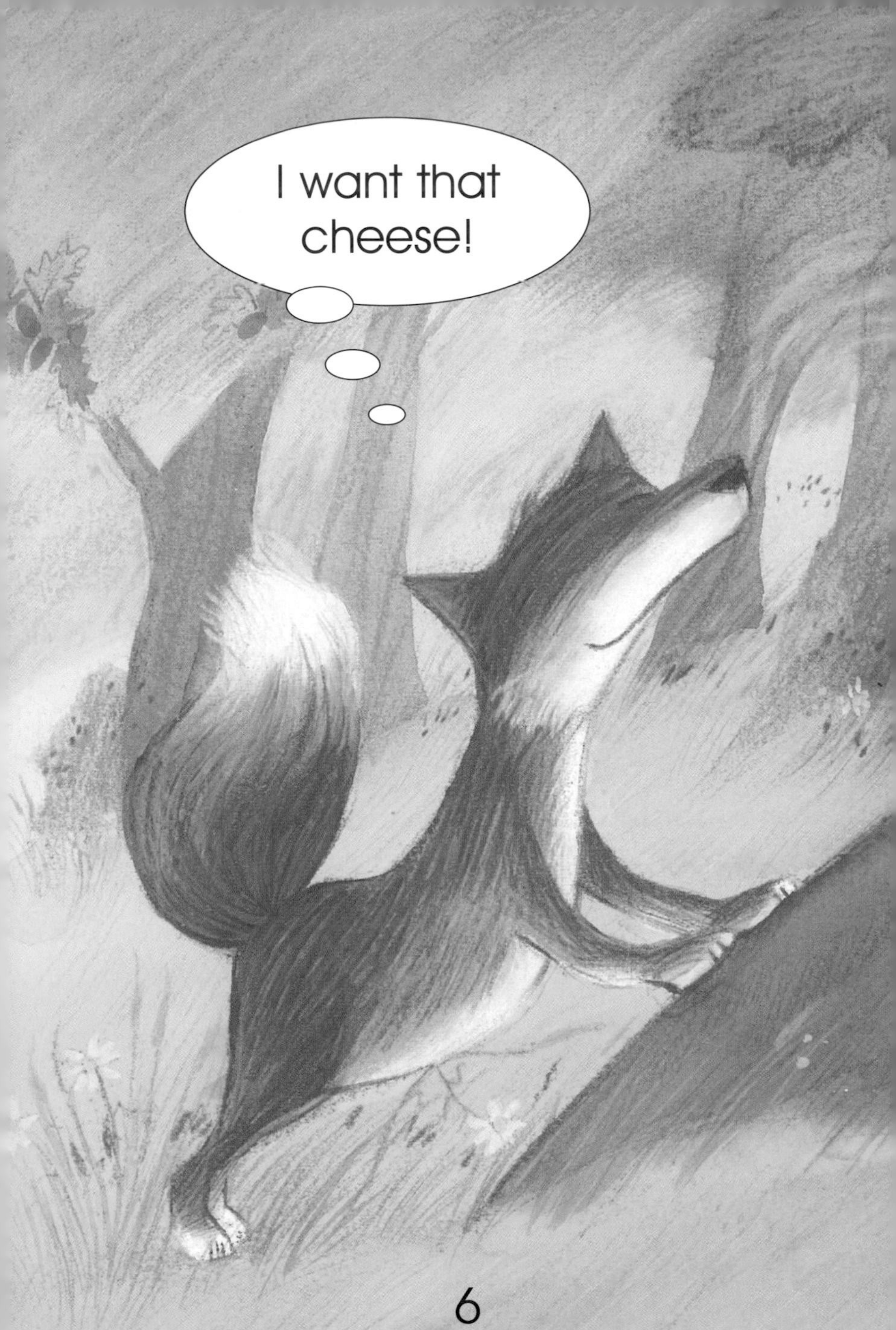
I want that cheese!

He grinned at Crow. "You're pretty!"

"What beautiful feathers!"

10

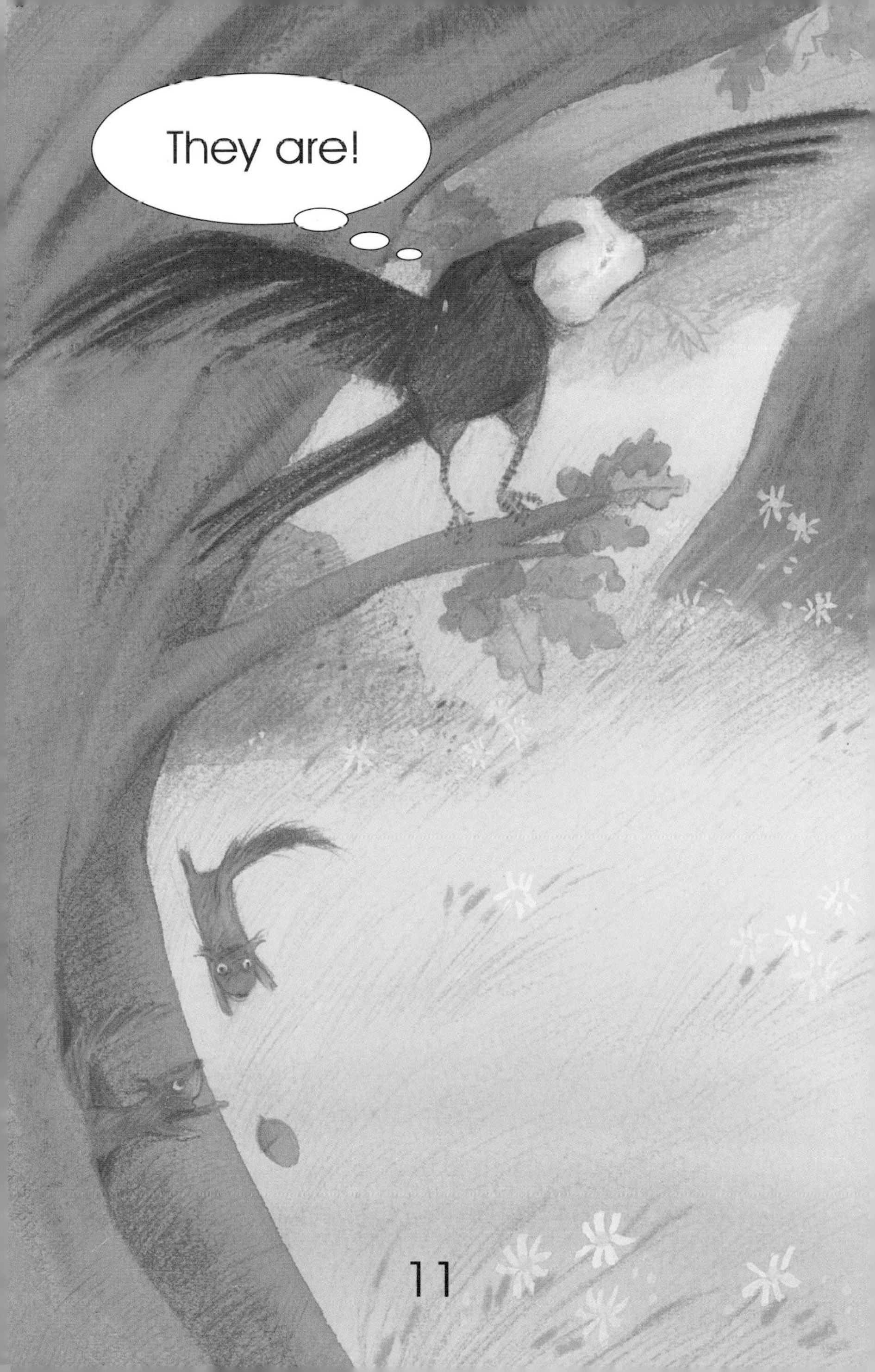
They are!

12

"Can you sing too?"
he asked.

Crow nodded.

She opened her beak...

CAW!

Down fell
the cheese.

Fox snapped it up.

19

"That was mine!"
cried Crow.

Fox
laughed.

"Don't always believe people who say nice things," he said.

"Sometimes they just want something from you."

23

Puzzles

Puzzle 1

Put the story in order.

A

"You're pretty!"

B

"That was mine!"

C

"I want that cheese!"

D

"CAW!"

E

"Can you sing, too?"

Puzzle 2

Find these
things in
the picture:

carrot

squirrels

mice

butterfly

rabbits

Fox

bees

27

Puzzle 3
True or false?

Fox is hungry.

Crow is pretty.

C

Fox is truthful.

D

Crow is clever.

E

Fox is happy.

F

Crow is happy.

Answers to puzzles

Puzzle 1

C

"I want that cheese!"

A

"You're pretty!"

E

"Can you sing too?"

D

"CAW!"

B

"That was mine!"

Puzzle 2

squirrels

bees

Fox

rabbits

carrot

mice

butterfly

Puzzle 3

A  B 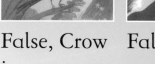 C

True, Fox <u>is</u> hungry.

False, Crow is <u>not</u> pretty.

False, Fox is <u>not</u> truthful.

D  E F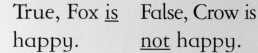

False, Crow is <u>not</u> clever.

True, Fox <u>is</u> happy.

False, Crow is <u>not</u> happy.

About the story

The Fox and the Crow is one of Aesop's Fables, a collection of stories first told in Ancient Greece around 4,000 years ago. The stories always have a "moral" (a message or lesson) at the end.

31

Series editor: Lesley Sims

Designed by Non Figg

First published in 2007 by Usborne Publishing Ltd., Usborne House,
83-85 Saffron Hill, London EC1N 8RT, England. www.usborne.com
Copyright © 2007 Usborne Publishing Ltd.